YOUTH SERVICES

WITHDRAWN

ZZZzNG! ZZZzNG! ZZZzNG!

a Yoruba tale

retold by
Phillis Gershator

illustrated by
Theresa Smith

Orchard Books   New York

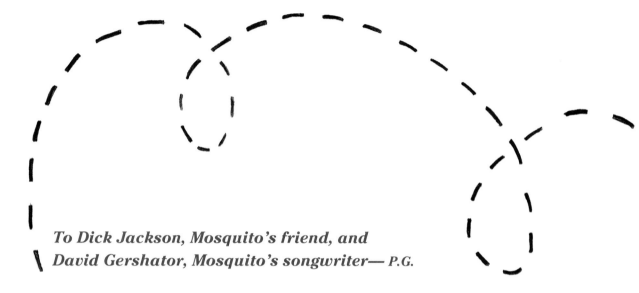

To Dick Jackson, Mosquito's friend, and
David Gershator, Mosquito's songwriter— *P.G.*

Dedicated to Jennifer, Emily, Eric, Austin,
Dillon, and Sawyer—*T.S.*

We gratefully acknowledge permission to quote from *Things Fall Apart* by Chinua Achebe, published by
Heinemann Educational Publishers, in the Author's Note.

Orchard Books, 95 Madison Avenue, New York, NY 10016

Manufactured in the United States of America. Printed by Barton Press, Inc. Bound by Horowitz/Rae.
Book design by Mina Greenstein. The text of this book is set in 20 point Clarendon.
The illustrations are pastel and crayon.   10 9 8 7 6 5 4 3 2 1

Library of Congress Cataloging-in-Publication Data
Gershator, Phillis. Zzzng! zzzng! zzzng! : a Yoruba tale / retold by Phillis Gershator ;
pictures by Theresa Smith.   p.   cm.
Summary: When Ear, Leg, and Arm refuse to marry Mosquito, she
shows them that she is not to be ignored.
ISBN 0-531-09523-1—ISBN 0-531-08873-1 (lib. bdg.)
[1. Mosquitoes—Folklore. 2. Yoruba (African people)—Folklore.
3. Folklore—Africa.]   I. Smith, Theresa, ill.   II. Title.
PZ8.1.G353Z98   1998   398.24'525771—dc20   [E]   95-51565

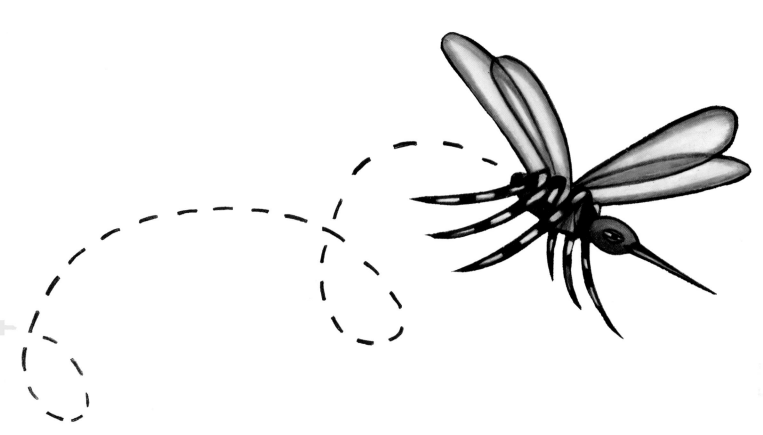

Author's Note

This story expands on a traditional tale, "The Mosquito and the Ear," from the language text *Second-Year Yoruba* by Hans Wolff (African Studies Center, Michigan State University, 1964). The story of Mosquito and Ear is also recounted in chapter nine of Chinua Achebe's classic novel *Things Fall Apart*: "Mosquito… had asked Ear to marry him, whereupon Ear fell on the floor in uncontrollable laughter. 'How much longer do you think you will live?' she asked. 'You are already a skeleton.' Mosquito went away humiliated, and any time he passed her way he told Ear that he was still alive."

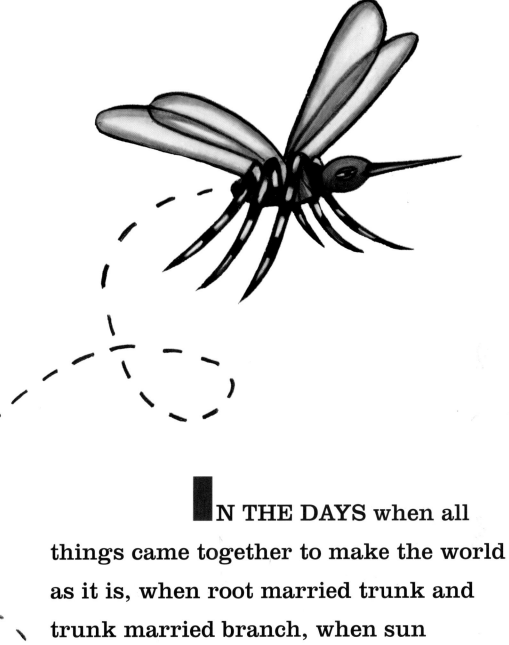

IN THE DAYS when all things came together to make the world as it is, when root married trunk and trunk married branch, when sun married day and moon married night, so it was for the animals too.

That is why Mosquito flew around looking for someone to marry.

She admired Ear most of all. Ear had a handsome
shape. Mosquito talked sweetly to Ear and sang a
joyful song:

"Here I come   *zzzum-zzzum*

to hum   *zzzum-zzzum*

and sing   *zzzng-zzzng*

rain or shine   *zzzng-zzzng*

I'm yours   *zzzng-zzzng*

if you're mine   *zzzng-zzzng.*

Let us marry,

marry,

marry!"

But Ear glanced at Mosquito and said, "Mosquito, go look for someone else to marry. You don't please me. You're so small and weak, you won't last in this world at all.

"I'm going to marry someone round and clever," said Ear. "I'm going to marry Head!"

Mosquito was disappointed, and her feelings were hurt. She flew around sadly, crying,

"Zzzng-zzzng, zzzng-zzzng."

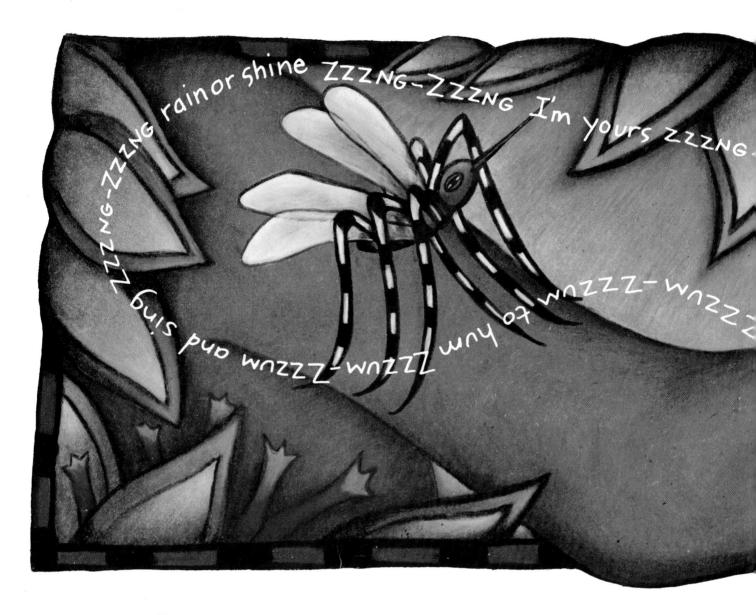

Then Mosquito saw Arm. Arm was as handsome as Ear. He had long, lovely fingers. Mosquito tickled Arm with her six skinny legs and sang a joyful song:

"Here I come   *zzzum-zzzum*

       to hum   *zzzum-zzzum*

          and sing   *zzzng-zzzng*

rain or shine   *zzzng-zzzng*

I'm yours   *zzzng-zzzng*

if you're mine   *zzzng-zzzng.*

Let us marry,

marry,

marry!"

But Arm brushed Mosquito away and said, "Mosquito, go look for someone else to marry. You don't please me. You're so small and weak, you won't last in this world at all.

"I'm going to marry someone big and solid," Arm said. "I'm going to marry Chest!"

Mosquito was disappointed, and her feelings were hurt. She flew around sadly, crying,

"Zzzng-zzzng, zzzng-zzzng."

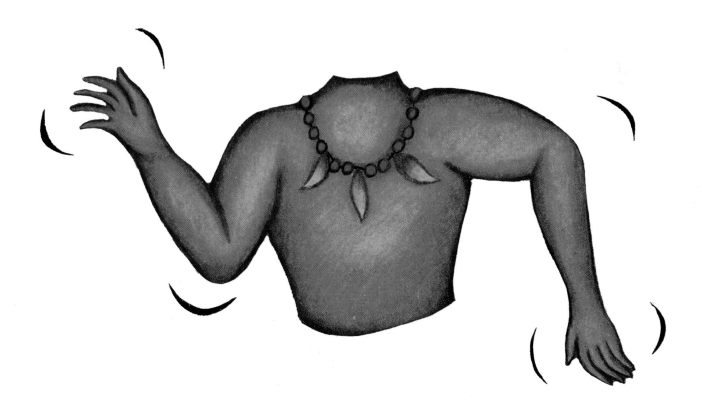

Here I come zzzum-zzzum to hum

Then Mosquito saw Leg. Leg was as handsome as Arm. He moved so gracefully, and he had five pretty, round toes at the end of his foot. Mosquito perched on Leg's ankle and sang a joyful song:

"Here I come   *zzzum-zzzum*

       to hum   *zzzum-zzzum*

          and sing   *zzzng-zzzng*

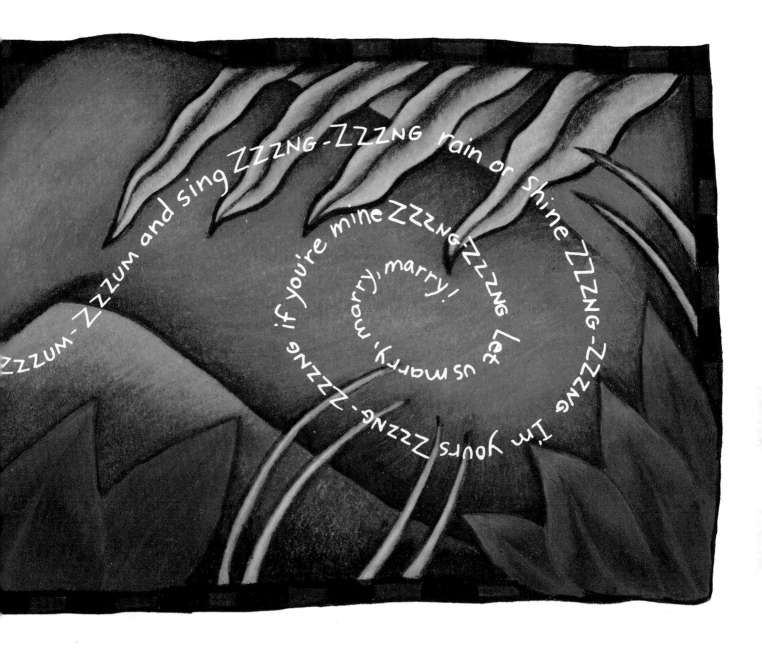

rain or shine   *zzzng-zzzng*

  I'm yours   *zzzng-zzzng*

   if you're mine   *zzzng-zzzng.*

    Let us marry,

     marry,

      marry!"

But Leg shook Mosquito off his ankle and said, "Mosquito, go look for someone else to marry. You don't please me. You're so small and weak, you won't last in this world at all.

"I'm going to marry someone strong and full of rhythm," said Leg. "I'm going to marry Hips!"

Mosquito was disappointed, and her feelings were hurt, and she was very, very angry.

"Ear and Arm and Leg think I'm small and weak. They think I won't last in this world at all. Well, I'll show them!"

And the next time she saw Leg, Mosquito sang an angry song:

"At night   *zzzng-zzzng*

I'll bite   *zzzng-zzzng*

    deep, deep   *zzzng-zzzng*

        in your sleep   *zzzng-zzzng*

            bite-bite   *zzzng-zzzng*

                bite-bite   *zzzng-zzzng*

                    STING-STING!"

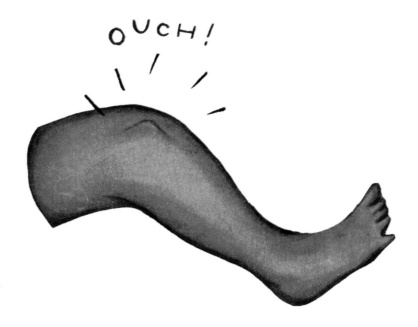

Mosquito bit Leg as hard as she could on his knee and made a big, ugly bump.

Leg said, "Look at that. Mosquito is still around in this world, and what a bite she took! Mosquito is stronger than I thought!"

The next time Mosquito saw Arm, she sang an
angry song:

"At night   *zzzng-zzzng*

I'll bite   *zzzng-zzzng*

deep, deep   *zzzng-zzzng*

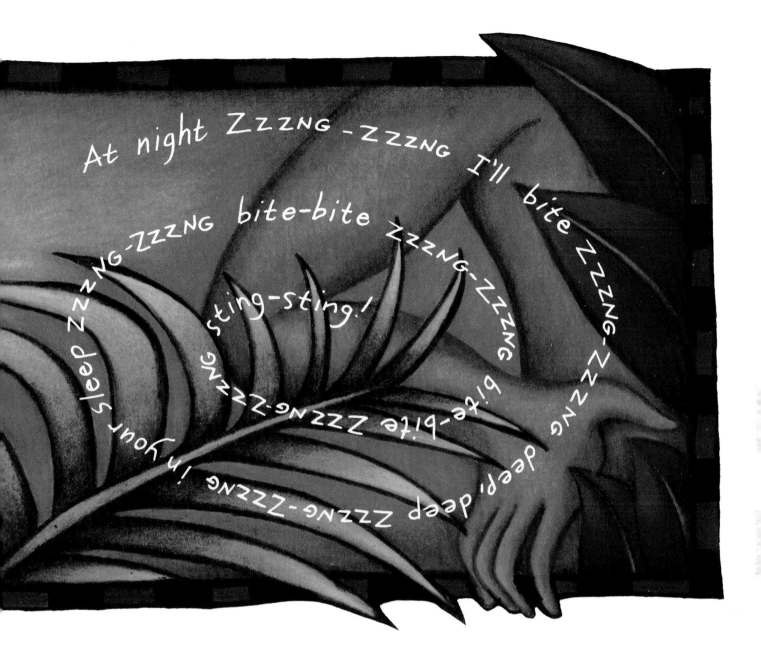

in your sleep   *zzzng-zzzng*

bite-bite   *zzzng-zzzng*

bite-bite   *zzzng-zzzng*

STING-STING!"

Mosquito bit Arm on one of the lovely fingers of his hand. It made him itch and scratch, and he cried, "Look at that. Mosquito is still around in this world, and what a bite she took! Mosquito is too quick for me!"

Mosquito didn't bite Ear, but she buzzed
"ZZZNG-ZZZNG" all the time, even when Ear
was trying to sleep.

"Are you listening, Ear?

ZZZNG-ZZZNG, ZZZNG-ZZZNG.

I'm still around in this world!"

Finally, Mosquito found someone to marry who thought she was just right.

"You please me a lot," her husband said. "You're big and strong, and I like your music too."

But by then, Mosquito was in the habit of biting Arm and Leg and buzzing Ear, and her children learned to do the same. *Buzz, bite. Bite, buzz.* And what do you think Mosquito and her children do, to this very day?

BUZZ AND BITE! BITE AND BUZZ!

"*ZZZNG-ZZZNG,*" they go, from ear to ear, singing Mosquito's song. "Here I am, and I'm still around!

"*ZZZNG-ZZZNG, ZZZNG-ZZZNG.*"